Stingrays

BY ELIZABETH RAUM

AMICUS HIGH INTEREST • AMICUS INK

Amicus High Interest and Amicus Ink are imprints of Amicus
P.O. Box 1329, Mankato, MN 56002
www.amicuspublishing.us

Library of Congress Cataloging-in-Publication Data
Raum, Elizabeth.
Stingrays / by Elizabeth Raum.
pages cm. – (Poisonous animals)
Summary: "This photo-illustrated book for elementary readers describes the venomous stingray. Readers learn how these ocean animals use the stinger on their tails to defend against predators. Also explains the threat of these stings to humans and what to do when they are encountered"– Provided by publisher.
Audience: K to grade 3.
Includes bibliographical references and index.
ISBN 978-1-60753-789-2 (library binding)
ISBN 978-1-60753-888-2 (ebook)
ISBN 978-1-68152-040-7 (paperback)
1. Stingrays–Juvenile literature. I. Title.
QL638.8R38 2016
597.3'5–dc23
2014038744

Editor: Wendy Dieker
Series Designer: Kathleen Petelinsek
Book Designer: Heather Dreisbach
Photo Researcher: Derek Brown

Photo Credits: Alamy/David Fleetham 14; Alamy/FirstShot 6; Alamy/Nature Picture Library 5; Alamy/WaterFrame cover; Corbis/Bernard Radvaner 26–27; Corbis/Dave Fleetham/Design Pics 20–21; Corbis/Macduff Everton 10; Shutterstock/Achimdiver 29; Shutterstock/Chatchai Kritsetsakul 12–13; Shutterstock/Daleen Loest 17; Shutterstock/iliuta goean 9; Shutterstock/Rich Carey 18; Shutterstock/Shane Gross 22; Shutterstock/vector photo video 25

Printed in Malaysia

HC 10 9 8 7 6 5 4 3 2 1
PB 10 9 8 7 6 5 4 3 2 1

Table of Contents

An Ocean Glider

A stingray glides through the ocean. Then it sinks to the sandy bottom. It lies as flat as a rug. A swimmer wades into the water. He steps on the stingray. The stingray whips its tail. A sharp **barb** on the tail hits the swimmer's leg. The swimmer screams. "Help! Help!" The ray swims away.

Stingrays glide through the ocean near the sea floor.

A stingray whips its long tail when it is frightened.

Q What does the venom do?

A lifeguard runs to help. The swimmer's foot is bleeding. A barb broke off in the wound. It has **venom**, a kind of poison. The lifeguard pulls out the barb. She stops the bleeding. She soaks his foot in hot water. The swimmer will have to see a doctor. He will probably get better soon.

A It attacks the nerves and causes pain. It may damage the heart and lungs, too.

Rays swim in warm waters near shore. They are very peaceful animals. They don't attack people. Rays sting only when they are scared.

Seal Beach in California is home to about 16,000 rays. More than 400 people are stung there each year. Most are people who accidentally step on a stingray. Most stings are not deadly.

Q I don't want to get stung at the beach. What can I do?

Stingrays blend in with the ocean floor. It's hard to see them.

A Do the "stingray **shuffle**." Don't walk. Shuffle. Rays will swim away.

Four stingrays swim in warm water near the beach.

Stingrays Up Close

There are more than 90 different **species** of stingrays. Some are big. The biggest grow up to 14 feet (4 m) long from the head to the end of the tail. That is longer than a large van! Big rays can weigh over 750 pounds (340 kg). That is more than four men. Many rays are smaller. The smallest kinds of rays are only 8 to 9 inches (20 to 23 cm) long.

Big or small, all stingrays have flat bodies. They flap their fins to swim. They glide along the ocean floor. Their eyes are on the top of their bodies so they can see above them. Their mouths are on the bottom of their bodies. So are their **gills**.

Look at the bottom of a stingray. Its gills make a V-shape under the mouth.

Sharp barbs break off in the enemy's wound.

Q Can a stingray's venom kill people?

Stingrays have long tails. The tail has a stinger with a sharp barb. Some rays have more than one barb. Barbs are made of a soft bone-like material. Up close, they look like saws. Barbs make deep cuts. They send venom into the wound.

A It can. But only 17 people have ever died from ray stings.

A Sandy Lunch

Rays eat worms, shrimp, clams, and small fish. These **prey** live on the bottom of the ocean. They hide in the sand. When a ray swims over the ocean floor, they also swim over their prey. The ray's mouth has special **sensors**. The sensors feel a kind of electric charge when prey is nearby.

Q Do other fish have sensors that feel electric charges from other fish?

This bat ray's snout wrinkles up when it opens its mouth to eat.

A Sharks do. Rays and sharks are cousins.

A stingray flaps its fins to stir up sand. They find food in the sand.

Q Do rays sting their prey?

Rays use their fins to uncover the prey. Sometimes they suck the sand into their mouths. They suck in prey, too. A ray's teeth form flat, hard plates. Rays use these hard plates to crush the prey. They eat the tasty bits and spit out the rest.

A No. Rays sting only for protection.

Watch for Enemies!

Rays use their eyes to look for **predators**. They use their tails to fight their enemies. Sometimes it works. Sometimes it does not. So rays hide. Most rays have dark tops. Some have spots. The spots look like shadows. From above, rays are hard to see.

A stingray hides in the sand.

Hammerhead sharks hunt for stingrays.

Q Do other animals eat stingrays?

A hammerhead shark sees a ray. Even though they are cousins, sharks eat rays. The shark hits the ray with its head. The ray falls to the ocean floor. The shark pins the ray down. The ray cannot move. It cannot sting. The shark bites the ray. It dies. And the shark gulps it down.

A Yes. Seals and sea lions also attack rays.

Warm Water Swimmers

Rays live in most of the world's oceans. Some live in rivers in South America and Asia. They like warm waters best. When it gets too cold, they **migrate**, or move, to warmer water. They often live alone. Most of the time, they stay on river or ocean bottoms.

Q Do stingrays live near the coasts in North America?

Rays like to live in shallow, warm water near beaches.

A Yes. They live along both the east and west coasts.

Sea World and many ocean resorts let people swim with rays. Is it safe? Most of the time it is. Over time, the stingrays become tame. They do not act like wild stingrays. They take food from people. They seem friendly. At Sea World, handlers cut off the barbs. They want to be safe. But many resorts do not remove barbs.

Stingrays that live near resorts are often tame and friendly.

Rays are big and strong. Most are wild and powerful. People name sports teams after rays. Hockey teams, football, baseball, and swim teams are called the Stingrays. Fast cars and boats are called stingrays. But to see a real ray, visit a public aquarium. In the ocean, do the "stingray shuffle." You don't want to get stung!

Q How long do rays live?

The best place to see a stingray is in an aquarium.

A No one knows for sure. They may live 70 to 100 years.

Glossary

barb A sharp or pointed part.

gills Slits in a fish's body that help them breathe.

migrate To move from one place to another to find a better place to live.

predator An animal that hunts another for food.

prey An animal that is hunted for food.

sensor A part of the body that gets a signal of some kind.

shuffle To walk without lifting your feet off the ground.

species A kind or group of animals that share certain characteristics.

venom Poison produced by animals such as stingrays.

Read More

Arnosky, Jim. *Shimmer & Splash: The Sparkling World of Sea Life.* New York: Sterling Children's Books, 2013.

Niver, Heather Moore. *20 Fun Facts About Stingrays.* New York: Gareth Stevens Pub., 2013.

Zeiger, Jennifer. *Stingrays.* New York: Children's Press, 2012.

Websites

Round Stingray | Aquarium of the Pacific:
www.aquariumofpacific.org/onlinelearningcenter/species/round_stingray

Stingray | Animals A-Z
a-z-animals.com/animals/stingray/

Stingray | National Geographic Kids
kids.nationalgeographic.com/animals/stingray.html

Index

About the Author

Elizabeth Raum has worked as a teacher, librarian, and writer. She enjoyed doing research and learning about poisonous creatures, but she hopes never to find any of them near her house! Visit her website at www.elizabethraum.net.